Andre Solnikkar

Pestilentia Innamorata

or: Loves in Time of the Plague

A Medieval Mural

"Once a hole is gaping, it cannot but excrete lies –
the lies of fear, the lies of lust and the lies of the poets."

1

Once upon a time, long after midnight, the king sat in his damp little study, hunched over an edict which forbade the Plague to enter the realm. The preliminary rhetorical insults had been easy enough to draft ("scourge of all nations, arch-violator of all that is holy, vile harlot of decay" etc.), though he suspected that "miasma" should be included as well. However, once he felt ready to compose the document's main part, he heard the door open and closed his eyes.

"My lord," the queen spoke gently, "it seems to me that the Plague will make a prolonged stay."

After a pause, the king opened his eyes and turned to the queen, whose face was covered with a wet, sticky-looking glaze of red. She shook her head, making a sign with one hand that she was not afraid, and the candles flickered in response.

"No," the king finally replied in a calm voice. "The Plague will not stay long, my lady; be patient just a little longer. But now, please, let me finish my work, as futile as it is."

"You don't believe in what you're writing, and the Plague will merely find it droll. So why should people find comfort in it?"

"Because," the king sighed, "existence is not a level playing field of reason, but a crooked stage of on which to spout predestined drivel. What else can I do for my people?"

The queen gave a little titter. "Do you still fancy yourself a philosopher, my husband? You're not, nor need you be."

"Go to bed, my lady. I'll see you later."

"I'll wait for you. Don't worry."

And the king averted his face, ashamed of his tears as much as of his shame.

2

Meanwhile, close to the border, where the swamp met the steppe, there stood a small village whose doctor was a content man. His office flourished, his wife had been as attractive as his mistress was, and two of his three sons had grown into sensible, industrious men. It was only Caden, the youngest son, who caused him constant distress: "He cannot work, he cannot sing, he cannot even pray. Wandering as if in a daze, lost in wordless dreams, what good is he at all?"

The doctor, though wondering whether Caden was indeed his son, was not a heartless man, but merely a practical one. When Caden came of age, he was informed that, being of no other use, he was to be a shepherd. "Your strength might do a blacksmith honor, but the horses will taunt you, and as a soldier, your sword will inadvertently slaughter your friends. So go with the sheep and find peace."

Caden's reaction, if any, was not recorded. He went and herded the sheep. When, some months later, it was found that he had come to treat a certain sheep with undue tenderness, his father pondered the matter carefully, had the sheep in question slain and told Caden that henceforth he was to herd the pigs. "Your loins are fierce and your eyes are clear, but your mind is lost in wordless dreams. You cannot be praised, you cannot be blamed, your face is a beardless mask. So go with the beasts and remain out of sight."

Caden's reaction was not recorded. The pigs squealed in response.

One hot and humid summer noon, Caden, lulled by the songs of weary birds, fell asleep under the ash which grew beside the black swamp. How long he slept, he could not tell, but all of a sudden, he awoke, for the birds sang no more and the pigs lay bloated and dead around him.

For a long time Caden did not know what to do. He stood up, his body iced with sweat, looked around and listened to the leaden silence which had fallen upon the land.

And out of the swamp there rose a formless being which was like a billow of black smoke and like a shower of glistening rain, and it carried the stench of decay. And the being whispered, "I am the Plague, and I am lonely." And its voice was the wail of a child, the croak of a crone and the chatter of a rat, and it said: "This is the year when all things die and no man will lack companionship on their way to hell. But you, fair boy, being neither beast nor man, will be as lonely as I am. The only thing left to you is to stay close to me and to soothe and entertain me. Then I will be your friend and I will love you." And it engulfed the boy.

Caden's throat tightened as the world around him faded and a black, smoky shroud smothered his body. He found himself floating in a void, lost in wordless dreams, and he was shown wondrous sights which he could not grasp, until he was awake again. "Will you join me, handsome lad?" he was asked.

Night had fallen and tiny, twinkling stars rose from the swamp. Caden stretched, feeling strong and refreshed. And thus, offered a choice of whether to die along with the pigs or to accompany and entertain the Plague on her travels, he simply chose the latter.

3

All through the night, last rites were performed for the queen, with the king averting his eyes, the wailers hoarse and veiled mourners dazed by incense scent. But then, a portly monk stormed the palace, burst into the ceremony room and started yelling at the corpse.

As none of those present could understand his half coughing, half singing language, they all just stared at him. Clearly, the monk was distraught, desperate and angry, with his eyes red and spittle drenching his scrubby beard. Was he trying to ask a question? He kept yelling at the corpse for several minutes, and the corpse remained unmoved and the onlookers were as in a daze. It was only when the monk grabbed the corpse with both hands and, still yelling, began to shake it violently, that the two guards present grabbed him and pulled him away.

The king, his face of stone, his manner apt to soothe the dunce, rose from his knees and calmly asked what possible purpose this profanity might have. It seemed to him that the monk understood the question pretty well, but when he replied, it was in that queer language of his, raised brows and dancing shoulders indicating an unfortunate inability to talk, understand or communicate in any other way. Then, his presumed explanation finished, he tried to confront the corpse again, but the guards gripped him tightly.

The king stared at the monk, while mourners mended the corpse's coiffure. Should he send for an interpreter? In truth, he didn't even want to comprehend the madman, to bother with more nonsense. That edict wasn't finished, either. What use was it all? And so, in the end, the monk was simply given a loaf of bread and thrown out of the palace. Murmuring under his breath, clutching his loaf and swaying slightly, he stumbled through the nightly streets. Some claim to have heard him titter while others say he wept. Some say that pursuers were trailing him, careful to hide in doorways and shadows. At sunrise, the monk had left the town.

4

Caden's father, the doctor, was up early as always, humming and busying himself with counting his patients' souls. He was surprised to find his son at dawn, entering the room in a state of excitement. He leaned back, looked sternly at the boy and told him: "First button your shirt."

Caden did so.

"Now, this is better. What do you have to say?"

"Imagine, father!" Caden exclaimed. "I met the Plague! She spoke to me and said... – Father? Are you in ill health?"

For the father lay dead on the floor, his limbs contorted and his face all black.

Caden failed to grasp the full significance of this occurrence. He sadly shook his head, assuming the look of horror on the dead man's face to be a physician's natural indignation at nature overruling him, and went to bid the dog goodbye. The dog, its eyes filled with terror, gasped, spat yellow foam and dropped dead within a second.

"It is well that I am going," Caden said to himself, "for this is not a healthy place."

"But then," the Plague replied, "no place we go will be healthy. Come on."

And thus, they were on their way through dew-covered fields, Caden and the Plague, a gaseous, glittering cloud floating beside him, bobbing up and down in the morning sun.

"Which way are we going, o Plague?"

"I have no long-term goals. I am beyond time and space."

"Who is it who is sending you?"

"It's not that I'm sent – it's people who are calling."

"I don't remember calling on you," Caden mused.

"I have visited the world on many occasions," said the Plague, "and never have I been satisfied with the result. For the world is full of pain and sorrow: It overflows with the cries of pain, and the cries of pain are a pain to me as well. So I will end their torment. But unthanked I go to deliver them from the pain and want of their brief lives, that they may rest in peace. They call me cruel, loathsome, merciless. Tell me, what do you call me?"

And the Plague reached for the boy and ran gaseous fingers through his hair.

"I call you no such thing," Caden replied. "For I lack the wisdom to pass judgment. Must we not all die in the end? I can do naught but pity you."

Though whether pity would suffice to sustain a relationship he didn't know for sure, he was not one to compress worries into words. The sunshine tickled his neck and the world seemed fresh and full of joy.

And thus, Caden and the Plague went their way, Caden whistling and the Plague dreaming. And it came to pass that they passed two solemn priests. The priests, seeing only Caden, but not the Plague, blessed him, and Caden fitfully thanked them both. However, once they had passed him, they quickly turned around and dropped their solemn demeanor: One of them brandished a knife while the other one kicked Caden in the groins.

"In truth," the one who kicked him said, "we are not priests, but robbers."

The second robber said nothing, but merely eyed his knife.

"Ah," Caden said.

"It is also true," said the first robber, "that as a child in the woods I did believe in Good and Evil. I was told that Evil was a sweetness to be avoided, and that Good was to be recognized by its scarcity. But then, one night, amid flashes of lighting, I heard the Lord God laugh as he set fire to our hut. *It is I*, he thundered, *who tells Good from Evil. It is I*, he screamed, *who gives and takes*. And the flames shot upward in a mad spiral. I fell upon my knees in the dirt and ashes of what had been our hut, crying and pleading with him to spare me. And then the Lord God and I sat for hours in the smoldering ruins, hugging each other, tears streaming down our cheeks."

"I have no money," Caden truthfully said.

So the robbers searched the boy, stripped him naked and, finding no money nor anything else of value, proceeded to beat him up.

"You will understand," the second robber said, "that I am not good with words. How can I explain myself?"

Perhaps, Caden thought, given the nature of men, the Plague would not be such a bad companion after all. "Plague!" he cried when the second robber, following a shrug of apology, made a move to plunge his knife into him, "help me, o Plague!" And presently the Plague appeared, a cloud engulfing the robbers and sending them into violent spasms.

"Where have you been?"

"I come and I go," the Plague replied. "Neither here nor there am I, and yet I am all over."

The two robbers, foaming at the mouth, were writhing at Caden's bare feet.

"They did look like priests," Caden mused. "And one of them spoke well." He shook his head and turned to the Plague. "Being with you, I cannot be harmed. You are indeed good company."

And the robbers whimpered, their wounds glistening in the sunshine, while Caden dressed and whistled. To his surprise, his whistling was answered by a band of mangy rats scurrying around his feet. He squatted down and smiled at them. "Hello, my little ones! You belong to the Plague, don't you? Ah, look at the little paws and the pink muzzles! Oh, you must be famished."

The Plague giggled. "It seems you've made new friends."

And when the rats had duly feasted on the robbers, off they all went, a merry band. And where they went, birds plummeted from the sky and weeds went gray and bristle.

5

A black storm carried the stench of the Plague, hurrying to herald her arrival. "The storm is laughing," sages spoke, "beware of the storm that laughs!" And shivering villagers huddled together in the low-ceilinged inn, clinging to their mugs. "I don't wanna die," they said to each other, and downing scores of ale they bonded warily, for unity was the best defense.

"You know, she isn't far away. I can smell the Plague in my guts," the portly monk announced cheerfully and set down his mug.

"Don't say the word," the pig-eyed mayor hissed, fear in his eyes. "It is hurtful to the dead."

The monk, while grinning, snorted. "I will find her all the same, no matter how long it will take, even though the very pope has told me to keep still and not to interfere. You see, according to him, God is sitting in His cave and cursing under His breath, and who are we to argue with Him? Well, I will! I will also argue with the, pardon the expression, Plague. Am I not a learned man, and isn't that what learning is for?"

The mayor, unsure if he was to reply or even supposed to take it seriously, glared blankly at the monk, if indeed a monk he was. Drops of wine and crumbs of bread had found harbor in his scruffy beard. Was he actually wearing a frock, or was it an old sack? And what kind of accent was that anyway? "From where did you say you were coming?"

The monk chuckled, as if remembering a clever joke. "You have, without doubt, heard the tale of the inebriated gravedigger who was accidentally collected along with the corpses and placed in a dead-cart to be transported to the pit of the dead. But once thrown into the pit – you have to understand that it was the middle of the night – , the digger awoke and, to make the collectors aware that he was not, in fact, a corpse, he began to sing and scream. A tale about the origins of philosophy, I would say, not least because it's made-up. It is said that a cat sat at the edge of the pit."

"How is this supposed to help?" the mayor asked. "People are afraid!" And indeed, two peasants had already started a desperate fight, wrestling on the floor and screaming at each other: "It's you who will die! Not me! Not me!"

The monk shot a glance at them and furrowed his brows. "Should they not attack their wives in bed? Are these men still virgins?"

"The moon is probably to blame," the mayor said, just to interrupt the monk's babbling. "What will do you should you actually find the Plague?" he asked.

The monk sat silent for a moment. "I do not know. When I face her, I'll know how to defeat her."

The mayor shook his head. "In any case, I must go home."

"I'm grateful for your invitation."

The mayor glared at him – what the hell was that to mean? – and rose. The monk rose too, with a groan, and kept close to the mayor's back, talking and smiling all the time.

"The arch-heresiarch Origines," he said, "gave one reason for the existence of evil in the world, namely that, according to Plato's interpretation of the law, when the better things are destroyed, the worse are pushed to the surface. If anything in the world be, it is through its badness that all things have their origin in. Now we may ask, of course, what is good and what is bad, and whether we should not be more afraid of the good than of the bad – the latter being bound to lose in the end, as we're told? If we consider the question not as a jest, but as a riddle, we may – "

A hand fell heavily on the mayor's shoulder, and the innkeeper growled at him. "Surely you want to pay, Sir."

The monk froze. The mayor reached into his pocket, "of course, of course," when quite suddenly – or hadn't they noticed before? – the innkeeper's eyes glazed over and boils popped up all over his face. The mayor retreated with a scream, brushing the infected hand off his shoulder. He tumbled through the room, pig eyes wide-open in wild panic, bouncing off a corner, staggering into a group of howling men who scattered all over the room: One dying fool infecting the other, a contorted row of collapsing bodies making its way through the inn, touch by touch and scream by scream, until a heap of corpses piled up in the inn.

The monk, who was still smiling, realized that he was watching the Dance of Death: A highly symbolic spectacle, performed with commendable vigor, even though a bit obvious; only the innkeeper had been content to collapse on a table, in a puddle of spilled wine. Just why were they all acting surprised?

After witnessing the dance for a while, he finally thought of escape. This can be handled easily, he told himself. Turn around slowly, open the door, leave the inn, close the door and run. You have had much wine, but you are still able to move. Now slowly. Draw no attention to yourself. No eye contact. Now – go!

The door slammed shut. The village street was dark and wet. "Ah well," said the monk, swaying slightly, stumbling away from the inn's lantern, away from the screams, around some crooked corners, out of the village and across the muddy burial ground, where the black storm got caught in his beard and wrestled to free itself. "Why bother? Fate'll find us anywhere."

He turned his head, looking for shadows in the dark, then spread his arms and broke into a helpless titter. "And you too, my pursuers! Ever so careful to stay out of my sight, as if any creature could hide in this little cell called world! But I will lead you on a merry chase all the same."

A dog barked from afar.

"Right after I've taken a nap."

He looked around, searching for a freshly dug grave to rest his head upon, or at least a tuft of grass, murmuring to himself: "After all these years, what does one night more matter?"

He felt an obscure urge to urinate or vomit, but decided against either. He just lay down and whispered: "Please be quiet down there, will you? A little rest, my friends; an advance on eternity."

And soothed by the worms' whispers, he quickly dropped asleep.

6

That night, while Caden was asleep, the lovelorn Plague stirred and fluttered. She whispered and purred and cooed to excite him, and the grass of the meadow quivered in the rhythm of her breath. But Caden took no notice and slept on.

Thus, the Plague appeared as a noble princess, as a little girl with braids, as a voluptuous whore wrapped in the scent of amber, and she hugged his body and caressed his limbs and covered his face with moist kisses. Still, Caden merely snored.

With increasing desperation, the Plague became a man, a beast, an octopus, engendering fantastic limbs and orifices the likes of which the world had never seen. She oozed, she protruded, she throbbed. But Caden remained lost in wordless dreams.

Finally, she despaired and collapsed into herself, taking the form of everyone's mother, staring at the sleeping, smiling boy. Her head lay on his thigh and she cried bitterly, while the rats watched her in reverent silence. "My power is at an end with this boy," she fessed. "O handsome lad who will not love me, remain in your wordless dreams. All kinds of men have been with me: tyrants and hermits, villains and priests, lascivious nobles, strapping dandies, would-be martyrs, and sad and helpless fools. In vain I have tried to fill my days with their pleasure and to quench my thirst with their tears. For more than a thousand years I have been lonely, and I shall be lonely for many years to come."

Exhausted and bereft of hope, she fell adrift in time and space.

7

The monk, in his dream, was arguing with God. It was a pleasant dream, for God was a blithering cretin and the monk made his case with ease. He had almost left Heaven when he heard God wondering, under His breath, "whether that monk's ass is as wide as his mouth." Enraged, the monk was about to turn and retort when he awoke, his head aching and his clothes wet, still alive and still in a dew-covered graveyard.

The monk blinked, took a deep breath and glanced at the faint sunrise shimmering behind dark trees. It was going to be a fine morning. He yawned. I must go, he reminded himself, my quest demands it. At least I have a quest. And he rose.

"Won't you stay and follow the play?"

A bright voice startled the monk; he turned around and faced an exceedingly ugly girl. The girl, perhaps twelve years of age and of slight build, wore boy's clothes. A greasy felt hat covered most of her hairless head but still left too much of her pale face exposed, bloated and distorted by disease. Half-hidden behind folds of glistening skin, light blue eyes blinked at him.

"What play?" he asked in a cordial tone. "You're certainly up bright and early."

"The graveyard makes a sightly stage."

"But will the dead make a receptive audience?"

"Well, you are here," the girl smiled, and the smile made the monk avert his eyes. "And there is no fee demanded."

"But where are your parents?"

"Passed away and out of sight. I carried the corpses in the cart until the birds took them. Then the birds took the cart as well. But fret not: I'll be both pro- and epilogue."

A likely story, though an unlikely play, the monk thought. "What is the play about?"

The girl chuckled. "Ah, merely pleasant fluff: Man rebelling against fate, with twists and turns all through the tale. But let's not stall – the sun will anon elevate."

"The sun will anon elevate," the monk murmured and shook his head. But then, assuming that he was still asleep and dreaming, he made himself comfortable on an overturned tombstone and looked intently at the barren space which, marked by two wooden pillars of unclear origin, served as a muddy stage. He wondered whether there would be an overture.

Apparently, there was none. The girl simply cleared her throat, scaring a belated bat into a frantic flutter. She looked at the orange horizon – indeed the sun did elevate – and bowed to her audience.

"Thank you for your rare attendance. I will now, with your permission and for your education, introduce the play in brief."

She took a breath and raised her voice:

"'til fatuous fate forfeits applause
By playing to a charnel house,
Let's – "

But frantic yells drowned her: "That hideous kid! Get hold of her!"

"My name is Jen," the girl protested, then stared at the band of villagers glaring at her with animal hatred. She attempted to run, but found herself surrounded. "She's from beneath!" – "Yes, from beneath!"

"No, you idiots, I'm not!"

Then things happened fast for a second. One villager was kicked in the groins, the next one in the stomach. Clearly, the monk reflected, the girl (provided that she was a girl) was used to fighting for herself, now her teeth even tore at a thigh. Alas, there were too many of them. Her clothes ripped as she struggled to get free, and they pushed her to the ground. "Fetch some rocks!"

With a groan, the monk arose, plucking wet grass off his frock and glaring at the assembled morons. "People," he said and slowly stepped forward. "Good people, listen. Since you're still alive, go home and hide from the plague."

"Who're you, monk? What's it to you?"

He smiled. "Why this ungodly commotion? Has not Saint Paul admonished the tortoise: *Festina lente*, slower your haste? And the tortoise lay with a rock and was all the happier for it. As I've been appointed by the pope himself to sniff out the devils that roam the land, I will take this one with me to Rome, so that she may suffer according to her sins." And he grabbed Jen's thin arm.

The villagers, feeling vaguely betrayed, paused for a moment.

"Come on, hell spawn! Hecate's left you stranded!" the monk exclaimed and started to leave.

"Stand still!" a villager cried. "You're in cahoots with her!"

"You dare to accuse a messenger of the pope, nay, of God Himself?" The monk suddenly raised his voice in rage. "Me, who burned four score heretics just last week for violating the law of *acedia*? Should you not kneel and beg for mercy?"

The villagers hung their heads.

"Heraclitus listened to the cries of the frogs in the well, but he couldn't do anything to quench their thirst nor, indeed, save them from drowning, for they insisted on crying until their tears reached their chins. So he sat down and laughed. Beware that you won't end like these frogs!"

A villager tentatively lifted his head to inquire about frogs, but the monk's finger shot at him: "You above all! Down, presumptuous human reason! Ah, why am I wasting time with blockheads whom nothing can touch but clubs? Go home, amend your ways!"

And the villagers, depleted and perplexed, shuffled off into the sunrise, blinking in the knowledge that they'd just got away by a hair's breadth, while the monk, his hand still grabbing Jen's arm, stood like a statue for some time.

Then he sighed. "They're gone. Let's go."

"Where to?" asked Jen.

"Just away from the fools."

Jen grinned. "You did put on a splendid act."

"Don't tell anybody," the monk replied, "but I've never met the pope. And lucky for him that I haven't, for I'd give him a piece of my mind until he'd send his purported God to hell. Tell me, what did they mean by claiming you're from beneath?"

"They say that demons appear from beneath to spread the Plague on Earth."

"Demons indeed! Someone's always required to blame."

"Why are you helping me?"

"You remind me of my daughter."

Jen looked at him. "You have a daughter?"

"Well… Once, I imagined one out of a fancy. Alas, she ran away."

"You know, I could use an actor like you. You're slightly mad, which would prove profitable when playing preposterous and pointless scenes."

"Can't you write a better play?"

Jen shrugged. "Sales would plummet. We may need to perform dances, too."

Perhaps, the monk wondered, I'm still dreaming anyway. How can I tell what is true and what not? Are we entering a birch forest, or yet another dream? I do suspect it doesn't matter. "Where are we going?" he wondered.

Jen looked at him in surprise. "Why, of course to find the Plague! The play is meant for her, after all."

The monk's mouth stayed open for some time.

"Don't stare at me like that. Is it not obvious that the greatest actor in the world, i.e. myself, would wish to perform before the most powerful being in the world?"

Jen's hideous face turned to the monk. The monk felt an urge to apologize, but simply looked away. And up in the birch trees and down in the shrubs, along with the birds and the badgers, the pursuers were calmly watching them.

8

In silence, the king knelt at the queen's bier, and the bystanders saw reason seep from his mind, tear by tear. He kissed her dead and bloated lips. He rose, waved the mourning committee to carry on and coughed once or twice, denying himself a more detailed display of emotions. And then he went to his study and tore the edict to pieces, commencing to write it anew.

"Most honorable Plague," he wrote, "it is with joyful anticipation that we request the congeniality of your company. In a country beset by woe and despair, none but you can possibly prove to be a guardian angel, a helping hand, and an educator. In the realm of the spirit, your authority will be found among the most precious treasures, for it shall guide the wayfarers on their journey of errors, on the inescapable road to the abyss."

Disturbed by sundry screams from afar, he put the edict aside and issued a law against screaming, "for isn't life bad enough as it is? Lo, the treacherous tongue suffers the thwack of the thistle named pain and smites itself a wound. It is my expressed wish that that the screams of the dying be muffled, for they have nothing to say worth listening to. Go forth and gather rags." Thus, Mufflers came to roam the land: Stern-faced men who looked with suspicion into faces, wondering whether they showed signs of illness, ready to stuff their orifices with rags, mud and, occasionally, organic matter.

Then the king went back to the edict or invitation directed at the Plague, but felt a vital ingredient to be missing. He sighed and buried his head in his hands: Why couldn't he die? The queen's voice echoed in his ears while his eyes saw naught but their own tears. He felt quite sure that he was losing his mind. In truth, he set his hopes on it.

That night, a comely chambermaid was sent to comfort the king. "Dig your own grave, child, you'll need it," the king advised, and she broke into tears.

Then, a learned doctor was sent to tend to the king. But he failed to perform his duties when the king threw him out after learning that he carried no matches with him.

And it was that very night that the palace burned to the ground, along with the larger part of the library, an orphanage and two bordellos. The librarians, it's said, screamed loudest.

And while man-sized flames dashed screaming through smoke-smothered alleys, while survivors fought and clawed their way towards the town walls, the king, his face hidden behind the mask of some mythical beast of his own invention, watched from behind a corner. "All that I once possessed I consecrate to the scorching of the world, where the blind ones rule and the banished ones shiver. Smoke and stink and memories I'll leave behind me, for I have no joy now in peace nor in sorrow, but I hold out my hand to a god that is the god of madness."

And the king turned around, bumped into a scared woman who squeaked despite the rag in her mouth, and he tittered behind his screaming mask and wondered whether the gods had tittered in a likewise way after they'd created the world. At sunrise, he had left the town.

9

A rosy haze rose from the meadows as Caden stepped out of the river, his body glistening and his eyes agleam. He spread in the grass, and the rats' tiny claws itched his skin as they scurried all over him and rubbed him dry. Caden laughed. "Hey, that tickles!"

He leaned forward, picked up a rat and smiled. "I like your tail," he said. The rat sat up and looked at Caden, and then at the grass. "It's got a nice curve to it," Caden said, reaching out and softly touching the rat's belly. It twitched and hopped a little, then sat down and licked his hand.

"Your fur's so soft. It must have been with me, in my sleep, for so long." He took a deep breath and looked into the rat's eyes.

"Are you finished?" asked the Plague, a grayish sparkling cloud. "Go on and get dressed, will you?"

"My, you sure are a grouchy one this morning."

The Plague sighed. "Yes, I guess I am. I'm sorry. Dwelling in this world tends to do that to me."

Caden rose and buttoned his trousers. "But it's really a beautiful morning."

"It is," the Plague admitted.

"Something is bothering you, though." And to the rat he said: "Come on, I'll carry you a bit." The rat curled up on Caden's shoulder, chattering happily as it did. Caden watched its tail twitch and twist as it played with itself.

"Caden, I have been thinking..." the Plague began. But looking at him, she reconsidered, paused and said: "Perhaps it'd make sense if I took on human form. After all, this – "

Caden shrugged. "Sure, why not."

The Plague hesitated a bit. "Is there a special look you might, perhaps, prefer? Like, say, a blonde?"

Caden looked up. "A blonde what?"

The Plague sighed. "Never mind. Have fun with your rat."

And she turned herself into a middle-aged ginger-haired woman in a mauve tunic, smiling and seething and dreaming of death, while bare-chested Caden, handsome as sin, strolled beside her. Soon we'll reach our goal, she reminded herself, stay calm: Are not all things finite, especially this species? Yes, indeed they are, and yes, of course it is. Soon enough we'll all be together.

10

Gasping and panting, the monk appeared from behind a birch tree, looking inexplicably worried. "Is anything the matter?" he panted.

"No," Jen replied and smiled.

"Why did you run away?"

"I didn't. Why did you stay behind?"

The monk looked at her with a pained expression. "Is it not written: Rest today, make haste tomorrow? Do you know where we are?"

Jen looked around, still smiling. "Lost in the woods, I presume. No, actually I've been here before."

The monk let himself drop to the grassy floor. "If lost we are, we're close enough. I feel the Plague in my guts."

"You really can do that?" Jen asked while running her hands through tufts of grass.

"Indeed I can, though I can't explain it." And with mock pathos, the monk declared: "She sitteth on a throne of thorns, and yet she feeleth no itch. She hath one foot in hell and one foot in the heavens. She is a woman, but she hath no breasts. She hath only one eye that is as the sun, which hath the power of penetrating even unto death, but cannot endure even life's bitterness. She hath the power of life and death, but hath no power over herself. She hath no compassion for the young, and is very jealous of the old. Or so the books claim, anyway."

Jen grinned. "Tell me, sweet ham, why are you seeking her out?"

"Ah, there's no goal worth pursuing but the impossible one."

"I see," she sighed. "Have it your way: I won't demand your truth. Would you say that Raven's a better name than Jen?"

The monk shook his head. "Too dark and obvious."

"I don't like the name Jen," she said. "I want a name one would give a wild animal, a fierce name."

"Ishtar?" the monk suggested. "No, probably not."

"What's your name anyway?"

"I left it behind when I went on my quest. What about Saber?"

Jen laughed. "I do want a girl's name."

Suddenly the monk's portly figure stiffened and his eyes darted from one tree to the other. "Damn them, they're still following me!"

"Who is? The villagers?"

"No, a different, more dangerous sort of pursuer, whose origins or goals are unknown to me."

Jen looked around. "I can't see anybody. You might, perhaps, imagine them?"

"I'm afraid I don't."

And thunder rumbled from afar.

"What's that over there?"

"Looks like a burned-down hut. Lightning must have struck it."

"Still better than nothing!" the monk exclaimed. "Let's run!"

And they ran, and the thunder shadowed them, but the lightning showed them the way. And while the rain beat the leaves, they huddled in the dirt and ashes of what had been a hut, dodging the frolicking powers of nature.

"I wish I had some wine," the monk sighed. "Is it not said that when even gods and ghosts fail in their tasks, all one can do is drink and sing?"

"Please don't sing!" Jen begged, as the black stormed howled with joy. "Can you hear that tune behind the storm?"

"No," the monk said warily, wiping rain off his brow. "Let's try and sleep."

"You can't hear the call?"

"La la la," sang the monk and covered his ears. And the thunder roared over the treetops, and the bats dived into the storm. Jen gazed at the night.

11

At dusk, the burning town had stained the crimson sky. And when the mad king crossed the bridge over the river, a lust for blood took hold of him, and when he saw an old man eyeing his mask in fright, he jumped at him and brandished his knife.

"Old man, what are you glaring at?"

"Nothing, good mask," the old man said and shook with fear. "I'm just hurrying back to my children."

And the king bent over him: "But of what use is that? Time and space float and dissolve like sugar in wine. You are already dead, even though you haven't yet been born. You're nothing but a drop on the tip of your father's crooked cod, a sigh in your mother's sore throat. And yet the worms are standing in line, waiting for their feast to fester. Why should you dread your death?"

The old man emitted a kind of whining grunt.

"Denial is your coping strategy, even now, and idiocy the cornerstone of your existence. You see, there is a plague which has infected the world, the pestilence of faces. Do you fear my mask and what might lurk behind it? Oh, no mask can be as horrible as your shrieking meat mask, as the mad flicker of your clouded eyes, the gaping void of your jabbering mouth, the writhing muscles under your porous skin: A suffering corpse made to dance! Be thankful that I deliver you from the curse called hope, while I transverse this vale of pus."

"By God, you're mad!" exclaimed the old man.

"That may be so, or maybe not. No matter what, you can't be helped."

The old man's face took a look of pity. "If I have to die, so be it, for likely I deserve no better. But let it not be said I'd withheld salvation from you. Listen, then: Follow the river to a lake on whose shores there towers a ruined church once burned down by God. And the floor of its chancel bears a hole which opens downwards and through which folks throw food at noon. For it is said that when the hole is offered no more food, what is down will come up, to the detriment of both. But those who offer food will be cured of all their ailments: an advantageous occasion."

"This is both beneficial and intriguing," conceded the king, his mask remaining immobile. "Let me express my gratitude."

And as the old man's wrinkles were about to rearrange themselves to convey relief, the king's knife entered the old man's body and let his blood pour out on the stones of the bridge. And bathed in crimson and orange, the mask went along the river, and the fish eloped, leaving jagged ripples.

12

"Can't you help the Plague?" Caden asked. "She's always in such a bad humor, and I like happy people around me."

And the rats whispered to themselves, then nodded and scurried away to the Plague.

"Don't sigh," the rats said unto the Plague, forming a semicircle around her, and the Plague looked up, sighed and replied: "Ah, what else can I do but sigh, for the comely boy won't care for me."

And the rats suggested: "Level your field of view. Go and enjoy a lower heaven. You will know what food you crave and you will call it what it is. You will taste delicious cheese and delight in it. You will taste old wine and smile at it. You will gaze upon fields of roses, and run to them, mindless of thorns, and frolic."

The Plague sighed again. "And then, my little ones?"

"Then let us carry you on our backs to your destiny. We will break your spine, remove your backbone, rip out your sinews and muscle and fracture you to the absolute and you will finally know the freedom you have longed for all your life. We will fill your head with beetles and your body with mud. You will believe we have come to save you and bring you happiness. Your face will turn red and your eyes will grow large, this symbolizes your tormented and sinful soul going to hell. Your nose will grow small and pointed, and your mouth and your chin will be flat, while the ears will turn pointed and rosy. Unless you die in the process, you will reach your apotheosis as a rat."

"I'd rather not," the Plague replied, and the rats sighed and shook their heads.

"In truth, the Plague is beyond hope," they told Caden, and Caden shrugged: "Well, I've tried."

13

Jen kept walking through the night. Her footfalls became shorter and quicker. Her eyes fixed on the ground, she made her way through the forest, bursting through bushes, tripping over roots, plowing through dry leaves. When she heard the forest's wind rushing over rocks and the rustle of leaves in the undergrowth, she knew she her destination was close. Her head hurt, but her legs kept going, and she could hear the sounds of the forest getting louder around her. Then she stumbled, falling face first into the moss.

She opened her eyes. An old man was sitting on the trunk of a birch tree. But while his body was that of a man, his eyes were the color of the earth and not of the sky, and his feet were roots.

"Father," she said.

"I'm not your father. Have you forgotten?"

"And yet I'm back."

"And yet you're back, little one."

"Don't call me little. I'm not a child."

"Indeed your fate is worse than that. You shall be despised," the old man announced, "and hated by men and women, and toddlers shall weep in the night."

Jen replied: "I'll wear a mask."

The old man sighed. "Nonetheless shall you be slain by your own people and then devoured by vultures. No play-acting, no matter how accomplished, will deliver you from that fate. No dreams will change the world."

Jen shook her head.

"Behold the Forest of Dreams," the old man continued. "It's the graveyard of the survivors. Its trees are growing into caskets for those who've fought their fate." And he pointed to a glade bathed in silvery light. "Here lies the priest who killed the old gods, only to find that the new ones lacked gratitude. There rest the cave dwellers who perished when led into the world. And over there is the grave of the rat who slew a hundred pigs at the Battle of the Plains. No one remembers its name. In truth, I pray that my name shall be forgotten, too."

And the old man, his eyes inscrutable and his voice quivering, turned to look at Jen. "I mean well, little one."

"Will you let me pass through?"

And the old man, closing his eyes, vanished, while slowly and silently the specters of the dead rose from the ground like morning haze.

"Blessed are you," they welcomed her, "for there shall be a fulfillment."

"How shall this be?" asked Jen.

And the specters whispered to each other. "First play for us," they asked.

"Only a short one," Jen replied. "I need to take care of a monk."

"Does he know?"

"Very little."

"Show us, show us," begged the specters, "we've never seen a monk before."

"Indeed? Well, all right, but only a short improvisation."

And Jen ruffled her eyebrows, stuck out her stomach and puffed her cheeks. At first, she improvised lines just as the monk might say them, then she impersonated herself by hunching to look smaller, and rolled her eyes and smiled; indeed, she also danced. Rapt specters, translucent and wispy, sat perched on their gravestones, and their laugh was a gust of wind to blow the minutes away like days.

Jen didn't mind, for a white cat approached her, its tail erect. Its eyes looked up at Jen. A soft purr came from its throat as it reached up and stretched its paws out before her. Jen went down on all fours, and the cat tenderly pushed her face with its pink nose, and in her joy, she cried out. And the girl played with the cat, and the specters smiled upon them.

14

Wrapped in swaying heather, the church ruins towered over the lake, and lizards basked on the broken walls, warmed by the midday sun. The king smiled behind his screaming, though immobile, mask and went through the overgrown remains, for it was said that within the ruins, there yawned a hole to cure all ailments, and wasn't the world in need of a cure?

To his surprise, he found the steps leading down to the cave before he found the hole itself. "How's a juniper a disguise, old clod?" he muttered, then smelled the hole before he saw it, for a horrid stench emanated from it. The king knelt down and took a peek, his mask glaring down through the hole.

In the cave's center, below the hole, rotting fruits and bread were heaped, and in the twilight around the heap, there stood, lied and cowered about twenty apathetic creatures which, after a pause, the king recognized as somewhat similar in general appearance to young men and women. They had, it seemed, been raised like goats, chains leading from their necks to the cave walls. Their pale, unclad bodies were covered in greasy filth. Some of them moaned softly, others rocked back and forth. Their eyes shone like those of nocturnal animals, and their swollen, toothless mouths were wide agape.

"I didn't expect to find you here," the king admitted.

Some of the creatures looked up to the hole.

"You don't understand me, do you?"

And a few of them, to the king's surprise, nodded.

"Know then that I'm your king. Behind a mask I hide, for I'm ashamed to be human."

"You're mad," one of the creatures remarked in a surprisingly regular voice. "And yes, you're looking human."

"Oh, miserable creatures who see the shadows and confuse them with the things," the king sighed.

"Shadows are the essence of the things which cast them. The light merely lies. Why paint your mask in glaring colors if not to hide your core?"

"You defend yourself well enough."

"A few of us were taught rhetoric," the creature replied. "Others were merely taught to serve."

"What madman imprisoned you here?"

"Our father brought us."

"Somebody fathered you all?"

"Father he is rightfully called, for he is old and brought us here to protect us. He will soon return."

"I do not understand," the king said. "But be it as it may. I'll descend to your level."

And he went down slippery steps, noticing with satisfaction that all the cave dwellers have been castrated or likewise operated on. "Providence led me down here," he mused, "for here the sins of mortal flesh are punished according to its desert. Oh, why did it have to move, disturbing the majestic tranquility of seas and deserts with shenanigans, genitals and words?"

The creature he'd been talking with awaited him with outstretched arms. "Behold the scroll wherein is written the truth about this cave and the father."

"Ah," said the king after a short glance at the scroll, "thank you, but no. Truth is a blunt weapon."

And with his bare hands the king pulled their chains from the walls and, tying them all together, he directed the cave dwellers to stand directly in the shaft of light emanating from the hole: "Look up! Yonder lies the world."

And the creatures, listless as they were, shuffled uneasily: "We see much clearer now and wish we were still blind."

"I shall lead you not to freedom, which is a dream – not to revenge, which is self-betrayal – but to oblivion. Let what is down come up, to the detriment of both. Let us purge this world from those who dwell above and restore silence to the land. Limp along, enlightened ones, you martyrs of folly, pilgrims to the void: Spread your stink, make the merry mice scurry into their corners, for your body is nothing but an extension of your mind and your mind has been rotting since birth. Rejoice in your decay, for a pile of excrement causes disgust, but a mountain of excrement causes awe and, eventually, admiration. Who, then, is with me?"

The creatures looked at each other. "Do we have a choice?"

"Of course you have a choice," the king laughed. "You're all agents of free will. But I'm the one who has a purpose."

"But isn't the plague up there?"

"It is indeed," the king affirmed. "And it should be afraid of you."

15

Wandering across the heath, the Plague burst out laughing. "Ah, it's all coming together."

"What is?" Caden asked.

"One of our invited, bereft of reason and all the cheerier for it, is already making his way. Another one, meanwhile, is dearly clinging onto his muddled mind, a wet straw in a raging storm."

"So he won't catch fire, I guess," Caden mused, then squinted at the orange glow in the distance: "Is the town burning?"

"A cleansing doomed to failure," the Plague chuckled, though it was hard to tell whether she'd actually retrieved her cheer or was merely pretending. "I think I hear them scream."

Caden pricked up his ears: Yes, tinny squeaks could be heard from afar. "Shall we go and warm our hands?" he asked. "Devour singed treats after our hearts' desires?"

After a pause, the Plague replied: "No, we have an appointment to keep. Have patience just a little longer."

16

Waking on a cloudy morning, the monk found that he'd slept in a puddle. "How I hate nature," he groaned. Then he remembered the evening and, turning left and right, he yelled: "Jen! Jen!" Alas, Jen was nowhere to be seen. "Oh, I've failed again!" What could have happened to her?

In utter panic, the monk lost the hold on his mind for a while. Assuming that he was still dreaming, he asked the badger where Jen was, but the badger pretended not to understand. He asked the owl, but the owl just wanted to sleep and screeched profanities at him. He asked the villagers, but the villagers said: "You're the dog that took her away from us in the first place!" and went after him with torches and pitchforks, and in fright he kept yelling: "Help! Help!" and later, even more incessantly: "Get me off this pyre!"

Finally, the jays and the thrushes managed to wake him up. But presently, his mind drew horrible images of various catastrophes Jen might likely have suffered, in some scenarios escaping one calamity merely to fall victim to a worse one. Perhaps the pursuers took her, or the villagers? Wild beasts are always hungry, too!

In short, it was a rather nightmarish morning, and the monk was lucky that Jen simply appeared from behind him, her hands groping for trees in support, her eyes dim and milky, uneasily making her way toward him.

"Where have you been all the time?"

"All the time? I was away only for minutes."

"In your dreams you were!"

"While I have dreams, I don't confuse them with life. While I can't see, I can find my way."

"What happened to your eyes?" the monk asked, his voice quivering.

"I won't see much for a day or two. But I don't worry." She smiled at him: "I've been told that I'll manage to perform my play."

The monk cast a sad glance at her.

"Will there an audience as well?" he asked. "No, sorry, I should just shut up."

She stroked his head to calm him. "A play," she said, "is a cleansing thing, no matter who is watching."

And the monk looked down at his mud-coated frock.

17

All through the morning, the king went eastward, his band of squirting cave dwellers dragging their feet and wailing: "Why can't we go west?"

"The enemy rises early," the king replied. "Cast your shadows against the sun, so to trap them in wild panic."

"We're tired," they moaned. "And we're not sure where we're going. If only our father were here!"

"Ah, think not that the range of bothers is limited in any way. Who is afflicted with common maladies may call himself lucky, for he'll find comfort in company. In truth, there are annoyances so *specific* that they will visit only one or two men in a generation, leaving them skewed and sick, and they are not listed in the wise books and leave the sages shrugging, and nothing can be done."

The loquacious creature nodded. "Ah, how I know this to be true. And yet, God has said..."

"God lied," the king replied. "And herein lies his greatest mercy. He has created man, a perambulating pestilence, poisoning itself, just as he poisons himself through the world. To spread the plague, he merely needs to pop the boil. But lo, in his infinite mercy he keeps a veil of ignorance wrapped around our eyes so that we may endure our lives."

"But through this very insight you see the selflessness of his grace, and you're be blessed with the holy horror of knowledge."

And the mad king laughed. "Splendid retort! And to think that serious men talk just like this!"

"Do they?"

"Oh, they're even worse, I assure you."

18

And when they'd walked for three days and three nights, Jen and the monk beheld a young man approaching them, clad like a shepherd and silhouetted by the sun, and a compact, mauve cloud bobbed up and down beside him.

"Now watch me," said the monk and coughed. "Visions may tell you to believe in your play, but I'll put on a show before your eyes."

"You think this is..."

"Yes, I'm sure."

And when the man and the cloud had come close enough, the monk said: "I salute you, o Pestilentia, as well as your companion."

And Caden said "Good evening", then cast a glance at the Plague.

The Plague assumed the form of an old maid just to shake her head. "Ah, he's not for me," she said.

The monk was speechless for a moment. "What? But this casual dismissal is highly insulting!" he then protested. "Have I not come from afar just to pay my respects?"

"Why do you haunt me, chubby specter?" the Plague asked. "Your jests don't tickle me."

The monk sighed, then nodded as if in agreement. "Yes, I think I'll go with you. Thank you for bearing with me."

Jen cast an apologetic glance at the Plague who, shaking her head, went on walking, with the others following.

"You see," the monk said, "even as a little child, what men did struck me as grotesquely amusing. But, when I laughed, the adults beat me, locked me up and looked so serious all the time that I had to run away, for how could I stop laughing?"

"Didn't the beating hurt?" Caden inquired. "They must have done it wrong."

"Ah, it hurt well," the monk retorted. "Indeed, I cried as well. But how could anyone not see that mankind is a sorry joke, that Dame Folly put bells around our necks to warn the cosmos in advance? That's when I swore to myself that never again would I utter a deep thought, unless I had it skewed and turned it inside out."

"Tell me, monk, have you no name?"

"To uproot oneself, the name is the first thing to forsake."

"Then I will call you monk," Caden smiled. The monk just rolled his eyes.

"Must you always play the fool?" the Plague asked.

"Oh yes," replied the monk solemnly. "This is my vocation, and I can have no other."

"One can both play a fool and yet be one," the Plague remarked acidly.

"And to be aware of that, is it not true wisdom?"

"No, it's not!" the Plague exclaimed with mounting anger. "Why should it be? That makes no sense at all!"

The monk smiled, as if he'd proved his point.

19

Lurching through smoldering ruins, the townspeople distracted themselves by disagreeing about the ways of the world, the traits and whimsies of the gods, and whether they were being punished or mocked by the Plague.

"Death is merely a deficiency of belief in life," a council claimed. "The Plague represents our own spiritual weakness. We've lost the trust we had when we were children."

"So you're saying," another one replied, "that it's wrong to grow up?"

"Let us not fight! We're all in this together!"

"No, we're not. Can't you see the population falling into ever tinier groups? What with flagellants mocking penitents and vice versa, the sick comparing their respecitve boils, the unaffected counting deceased family members, people calling for random justice and the destruction of all but their own homes? The prices for well-poisoning have risen again!"

"But how can this surprise anyone but a – "

"Gentlemen, please!" the burgomaster exclaimed.

"Burgomaster, there's a man with a mask outside."

"Another plague quack?"

But the king had already entered the office.

"Good morning, gentlemen. I came to tell you that you'll die."

"You're mad."

"In truth, I'm tired of hearing that line."

"Then why do you wear this mask?"

The king sighed. "Never mind. Just know that my army of troglodytes is waiting for my signal to lay siege to your ruins."

"And... why?"

"Without aim we wander in a fenced garden, and screaming blooms we pluck." And the king sighed and turned to the door. "I'm not a cruel man, that's why I offer you a chance to repent, to pray perhaps? No, better be merry and mirthful."

"Sure, sure," said the burgomaster. "But in truth, we've survived the

plague, so we'll likely survive a masked madman."
"In two hours we'll attack!"
"Stop screaming, or the Mufflers will get you."

And the king, enraged by this dismissal, held a speech to the drooling creatures: "And while the town burned and men and women perished in heaps, I still found survivors walking around. And I said unto myself: *Vos facti pestem*. You must become the plague – a new, improved plague, deadlier than the pestilence of old, with fresh, amusing symptoms twisting the cries of the damned into a jolly choir about values and choice! 'tis is the dusk of decay, and the maggots are crying: Soon, very soon! Let your minds be consumed with hate and sickness and pain! Watch the world growing smaller in response! Tear down the wall of flesh, my pretties!"

And the creatures moaned, and some coughed, and a few of them indeed limped towards the direction of the smoldering town walls. But instead of attacking, they stumbled and closed their eyes, and they bore the signs of the plague, covered with foul boils and screaming in pain and terror. Their faces, black and bloated, spurt blood, and their clothing broke in pus-drenched shreds as they clawed at their wounded flesh. Inside the town as well as outside, people dropped dead everywhere, until there were no more groups, merely a smoldering heap of fly-covered bodies, disfigured into eternal unity.

"Well, that I didn't see coming," the king mused.

20

While the monk was moping and Jen went away to rehearse her play, Caden cast his eyes over green pastures dotted with sheep.

"I wonder," the Plague mused. "What might happen on a hot summer's day to a stray sheep? Had not a hundred thousand sheep to die before one learned to jump?"

Caden smiled. "Gotta go for a minute," he mumbled and went off, dropping his shirt on the way.

"We cannot interfere," the Plague sighed. "I will not force my love upon him."

"What kind of love would that be?" asked the monk.

"What is the purpose of flesh? What is it like to bleed?"

"Are you making a pass at me?"

"My task is to vex the world with pain, to cast anguish and grief. It *is* a lonely job. But worry not, you're not formed from the matter of love."

"Thank you," the monk grunted.

Caden moved swiftly between the sheep, toward one specific lamb. He felt his blood boiling and he knew he was in love. His glistening body leaned over the warm, woolly torso. He grabbed the lamb by the collar and pulled it to one side, and it let out a surprised groan. Caden's breathing was rapid, and he whispered into the lamb's ear, "Don't be afraid!" And he embraced the lamb. The lamb's legs trembled, then gave away.

The monk shook his head. "A snake makes a woman sick; a fish makes a man mad. A snake is a beast with its tail between its legs, a fish is a beast with its head between its legs, and the man comes in a mix of both. So you get something like this on your plate. It's always either blood or semen, is it not? Things have genitals that shouldn't even have hands."

Caden, distracted for a moment, looked at him, wondering whether he was to say anything.

"No, my boy, I'm not blaming you. You can't help it – the time is out of joint."

"Monk, monk, monk," the Plague chuckled. "I reap, he sows. Is it not the natural way, as it's been since time began? Everything would seem to be in order – apart, perhaps, from you."

"Not only have we a Plague, we have one that makes smart cracks."

"He is the force of life, and how will you judge life?"

"He is a horny imbecile."

With a final wet, slapping thrust, Caden let out a guttural growl. The rest of the flock stirred as the bleating lamb galloped away. Caden's eyes glazed over and he let himself drop on the grass, panting and wiping squirts of blood off his face. "Now I will be lonely again," he sighed.

"I will take on flesh," the Plague replied. "I will form a mouth to kiss your bright body, and two breasts to suckle you. And I will scream with joy."

Caden smiled. The monk retched.

"I know," said Caden, squinting his eyes, "you're judging me. I don't care much about being judged."

"I apologize," the monk replied dryly. "Sometimes my envy gets the better of me, at other times my stomach does."

Caden turned his head. "Come over here, little Jen."

Jen came over, and Caden sat up.

"See that girl, monk? Isn't she misshapen and repulsive? And yet he has what you don't have: She has blood flowing through her veins." He kissed Jen on the cheek. "Her flesh will stir, her heart is like a bird in spring – while you stink of the pit. Have you ever escaped from it?"

Jen snuggled up close to Caden, but the monk tore her away and glared at him.

"Repeat after me, plague boy: My body is filled with all sins and desires of the flesh, and I have not known any thing good, to wit, truth, love, or justice. I am worse than the beast in the fields, more wretched than the worm that gnaws, more foul than the vomit of the dog. I owe my pardon to all the world."

And Caden burst out laughing.

"Don't touch the girl again," the monk growled.

"I'm not a child. Wait until I perform my play."

"What's it about?" Caden asked, but Jen just smiled and put her finger to her lips.

"Lucky lass, who has a secret you are wise to. Will it explain your face?"

The monk just groaned.

21

A trail of blood followed the few creatures who'd escaped their own attack. The king, behind his screaming mask, was groaning while limping back to the cave.

A creature's voice was quivering. "Most of us are dead; what remains of us will soon collapse. This is your work, mad king."

"The pure die first," the king exclaimed. "For only so can they stay pure, my poor, pathetic minions!"

And the creature presented, again, the moldy scroll.

"Will you read it now, perhaps?"

"My grace knows no bounds and my legs give in, so I will look at your truth."

He sat down in the grass and, peering through the holes of his mask, he read the title, *On the Expurgation of Evil*.

"A fairy tale? Oh well. Fifteen years ago," he read, "when the plague last visited our country, our late, wise king arrived at the conclusion that evil is an acquired trait, learned by observing the world. For the moment a child is ejected from the womb, its eyes behold evil. Only by isolating man from the world can he be kept pure at heart. And as the mind, likewise the body: Who shuns filth, will stay clean. From that it followed logically that babies needed to be robbed from their cradles, and thus, the old king commanded us to do before he passed away. And we took as many as we wished and locked them in the cage, and the people dreamed up conspiracies."

The king looked up.

"After the first step, the second one must follow: Complete separation with controlled affliction. Why do hermits drink snake venom? Why do peasants smear matter from a smallpox sore on the genitals of healthy cows? Clearly, these rituals are meant to confer immunity, just as intercourse is meant to banish death. Confront the body with a bit of disease, and it will be prepared for a full onslaught later: A species immune to all plagues and diseases. Alas, it takes much trial and effort to find the right amount of poison, and my prayers go out to those who perished or even, worse for them, escaped. Yet I endure and tend to them, for science never ends."

And the creature looked at him with moist eyes.

"What a joke!" the king exclaimed. "In truth, nobody is more susceptible to all evil than you."

"So it would seem," the creature said.

"Why didn't you tell me before?"

"I tried to, but alas, you're mad and we were too susceptible."

And the weak creatures took the weak king, and they dragged him up the hill where a single ash held wake, and they tied him up and hung him upside down from the ash's branches so that the devils might grab his head when they rose from hell. Then they made their way back to their cave, but collapsed long before: The king watched them tumble down, or upward, and he laughed and sang and wailed until the last of them had succumbed and the vultures settled on them.

And thus, the king hung upside down, with bloodshot eyes, night and day, slowly swinging in a gentle breeze.

"I really must say," he mused, "that I welcome my torture. Twisted and broken, I can see that nothing is whole. Worship me, for I see everything clearer."

"Sure, sure," said the vultures.

22

Silently, they made their way through the night.
"Are we there yet?" Caden asked.
"Soon, very soon," the Plague replied. "Just up the hill."
"Good," said the monk, "we'll see the pursuers better from there."
"Assuming they exist at all."
"Of course they do! Let me relate the truth."
Jen looked at him. "But why?"
"I must unburden, little Jen. Perhaps it's raw material for your play?"
And he coughed.
"Let me start where everything starts: In hell. Nobody understands the nature of hell. For instance, old wives of either sex insist that there's a Devil ruling in hell, but there isn't. Hell is, in fact, under liberal rule: The dead decide themselves and you can imagine how well that works."
"Well, now I'm curious," the Plague muttered.
"I like that," murmured Jen and took notes.
"Before you're born, you're predestined: Your fate is forged in hell. Make him a beggar, her a queen, this one a knave and that a dog: So speak the dead on duty there, and fashion you to life. Then you escape the womb, you live and live, and then you die again – to find yourself in hell once more, the worse for wear, and welcomed by your kin: Tell us, did you like the show? The gout worked out all right? Pity 'bout the cock, I'm sure. Next time, we'll change your role and fit you with another soul. So speak the dead, to take revenge, to sabotage the play called Life, in vain hope of escape. But it goes on and on and on, while God has long ceased watching."
The Plague made a sound like a rusty door opening for the first time in centuries.
"Are you laughing at me?" the monk asked angrily.
The Plague took some time to catch her breath, then took the form of an owl and exclaimed: "Confounded monk, you're a hoot."

"No, merely dead. You see, I ran away. Hell is perpetually drowsy, just going through the same old motions. It's the origin of the expression: Something is boring as hell – indeed, hell was created *out* of boredom. So I left, and nobody cared. And now I am looking for a proper, a final way of dying, of calling the damned play off."

"And how do you propose to accomplish this feat?" the Plague asked, striving to keep a straight owl face.

"Is it not obvious? God's the producer of the play, so it follows that he must perish. Enter his domain, o Plague, and lay your hands on him!"

The Plague sighed. "You know nothing about the world's inner workings. Worse, you know nothing about yourself, making it up as you go."

"I know enough to despise myself!"

"What a barren sentiment to cling to!" The Plague had taken the form of a crooked beggar woman and cackled melodramatically, showing a single tooth. "Imagine you've been fooled, o fool! Assume that you're still cozy in hell and have been all of your ostensible life! How would you, of all creatures, be able to tell a truth from a dream? What a boring liar you are!"

"I'm not lying: I'm patching up gaps in the world! And have I not done penance? Have I not walked among the sick for years? Have I not cast myself as every character in reach?" He dropped to his knees. "I even played the lover once, which in itself should grant me forgiveness! Why won't you kiss me now?"

The Plague sighed and plucked a flea out of her hair. "You believe the universe has been plotted and codified according to laws and reason? That anyone could grant you forgiveness, even though behind your myriad masks laughing at each other, there's none to hold responsible?"

"Who am I, then?" howled the monk, by now embarrassing everyone.

The Plague sighed and patted his head. "One thing's for sure, you're not a monk, even though you *are* amusing in your way. Now let's get up that hill."

However, at that very moment there was a polite cough and when the monk turned, he faced four intimidating men in black.

"Please pardon our intrusion."

"You're the pursuers!"

"We've been following you, but not to pursue you."

"But why?" yelled the monk.

"We needed to protect you. You see, the old king, intensely disliking his infant's incessant babbling, had decided to swap him with one of the newborns herded in a certain cave, and the changeling was brought up as successor to the throne. But when he began to lose his mind, it was imperative to find you," and the men bowed deeply, "for you, your Majesty, you're the rightful king."

And they prostrated themselves before him and held out a shimmering crown to him.

"This act's aptness," the monk replied serenely, ignoring Caden's laugh, "I can complement by renouncing the burden of my office forthwith. For I've been informed by a reliable source that I know nothing of the world – how could I possibly rule it?"

"But – "

But the pursuers fell dead before they could articulate their protest, and the rats scurried around them.

"Thank you," said the monk. "I couldn't possibly think of leaving you now."

"It was my pleasure," smiled the Plague. "Now let's move on: Our goal is near!"

"May I have the crown?" Jen asked. "It makes a splendid prop."

"Please be my guest. It's probably too large for you, but we can bolster it with twigs."

23

A star-bright summer night it was, and the sky was the same blue, the same gold, as it had been a thousand years ago. They all climbed up the hill where an ancient ash held wake.

"This," the monk improvised, "is the Hill of Truth. Or Truce. Some ancient chieftain's name, I guess."

"It's not," Jen grinned, "but I see your point."

And when they had reached the hilltop, they found a masked man hung upside down from the ash, tittering like an idiot. "So we've finally found each other," he said.

"So we have," the Plague replied. "You went through quite some trouble."

The monk looked from one to the other. "You know this man?" he asked the Plague.

"I knew his wife," the Plague replied. And the king tore off his mask with a dramatic gesture.

"That is the man who believed himself king," the monk whispered. "Better not tell him who he is, he's in sorrow anyway: The Plague has killed the queen." Caden shrugged.

"Nice mask," said Jen. "What does it signify?"

"Ah," sighed the king who wasn't. "It's just my vision of disease. And what is the disease? Passions like fear, greed and fornication dressed up as fancy lies: Truths, values, souls. And yet, even these diseases pale against the ills of the heart, the pains of loss, of fear, of finding no way through the void. But you, fair Plague, will save us all! Free us from these fetters of flesh!"

"That's why we were walking all the way?" Caden asked. "To meet another loony? Is everybody nuts?"

The monk, lost in thought, nodded quietly.

"Perhaps," the king said calmly, "you could get me off this tree before the apocalypse begins, if it's not too great a trouble?"

"Low-hanging fruits," the monk mumbled and went to work. After watching for some minutes, Caden pushed him aside and severed the rope himself. The king landed on his head.

The Plague rubbed her hands. "Well, it seems we're finally all together. For even though I didn't call for you, you sought me out by virtue of your hearts' desires, and thus, I greet and pity you. Let no one say that the Plague lacks courtliness."

She turned to Jen. "You, little dreamer, found me on account of hope," she said. "Even though you have not performed your play, you shall not be displeased by tonight's spectacle."

Addressing Caden, she smiled: "And you, comely boy, you live for pleasure, and pleasure you shall procure in abundance."

Caden grinned. Jen took notes.

"King, your pain is reeking to heaven. Of course you'd seek me out, and I shan't disappoint you."

And the king bowed his head.

"And you," she turned to the monk, "were carried by the wind of your fear, and loyal fear merits reward."

The monk opened his mouth, but said nothing.

"All of you, my companions, deserve my gratitude, for I will freely admit that I was beset by gnawing doubts, in fact: desires, from which only your pathetic existence relieved me. Worthy representatives of your species you are, and witness you shall bear tonight. And now, with your permission, I shall return to form, so that the play can commence at last."

"Am I too late to watch?" a toneless voice inquired, and a chill was cast upon of those present still human.

"Who're you?" the monk asked the black shadow who kept making vague motions over a white blur he seemed to hold in bony claws.

"I am the Shepherd of the Shades. I am the one who told you so."

The monk opened his mouth.

"Shhh…. don't wake the cat."

24

And the Plague showed herself as a black-mouthed monster whose body was a black skeleton filled with scabs, and it was hideous to behold. "I am the True Fear!" the Plague laughed, and she screamed: "I have come to turn the world inside out."

The monk couldn't help but smile.

"O Plague," Caden ventured to say, "are you quite sure you're fine?"

"I've never felt better, fair boy!" And with a raising of her claws, a black mist obscured the heavens and covered the land while, at the same time, water poured up from the ground, forming great mounds teeming with worms. And the gnawing of the worms was like a rustling or whispering too horrible to hear.

And the Plague said, "I am the one who made thee this mist, and it will cover the world so that we may have a shroud to frolic on, for I am the True Pleasure as much as I am the True Pain." And she embraced Caden, and Caden thrust into her, and she trembled, and whitish miasma streamed out of her mouth to smother the land and devour all flesh. And as the sickening fume rose higher and higher, the stench became so great and so overpowering that the soil cracked and the sky paled.

And the Plague said, "Let there be a hundred thousand sores in the flesh, the bones and the teeth, the hair of the head, even the nails of the hands and the nails of the feet. Bring forth my vessels of fear." And the sky turned crimson, and the dead rose from their graves and mumbled, in a hundred thousand voices, "I am the plague, the final plague," and their bones were filled with the sores of death.

Jen barely seemed to notice.

"Take note, little Jen! The play begins in earnest!"

"Please let her be," pleaded the monk. "Not her, just not her."

"I will not harm her," said the Plague. "Let her populate the wilds with unsightly kids and eagerly-staged lies."

"You're not really such a bad sort," the monk mused, and the Plague smiled at him: "Neither are you, in truth."

And the dead went forth to spread the Plague to all four corners of the world, and no man lacked companionship on their way to hell. And the firstborns of the dead came out of their graves, having their flesh ripped from of their bones, and they screamed for milk and pus. And Caden went naked among the soiled corpses, and whenever he found a dead girl with the eyes of a sheep, he would embrace her. And when he found a dead boy with the eyes of a deer, he would turn the boy around and embrace him. Ripping through intestines, his muscles tingling, his eyes rolled back in his head, he gasped and grinned: "It's like my dreams!" Black, viscous blood poured over his body and flowed down his legs as he went on.

"Is it not said that a straight sword has no place in an unclean sheath?" the king chuckled, then halted when embraced from behind.

"My husband," urged the rotting queen, "will you join me now?"

And the king turned and smiled. "So long have I been waiting, my lady. I nearly went mad." And he sighed and embraced her.

And the Plague laughed, and her laugh was an earthquake, and she cried, and her tears were burning lava. And as men screamed, Mufflers pursued them and threatened with their fingers, trying to stuff their mouths before they died themselves. And cadavers danced in the flicker of torches, and the worms rejoiced and the rats chattered and the vultures screamed in delight. How rapidly the eons passed!

In the end, Caden, hoarse and happy, caked with blood and semen, smiled and fell asleep. The Plague, arm in arm with the monk, went off to new adventures, and the monk smiled and sang. Death, stroking a yawning white cat ("Not yet! Not yet! Go back to sleep!"), tiptoed away. And silence fell over the barren, gray plain.

At dawn, Jen rubbed her eyes. For a few moments she looked around. Perhaps she shrugged, or the child in her womb might have leaped. Then, undaunted, her crown askew, she set off.

25

Caden saw that he was naked in the moonlight, and that the world was a graveyard. There was nothing but his heart beating, and the air. His skin was hot and clammy from the boils which covered it. He tried to move his hand, but it stiffly remained where it was, the arm bent in the shape of a snake. He felt the infection spread through his body, a tickle through a pulsing vein, a whiff of fire behind his eyes. All of a sudden, a sound came, like a sigh, and he closed his eyes and saw that it was a sound from inside him. It was a cry of pain. From inside his body he was screaming, and the next thing he knew he was falling onto the cold ground, drooling pus and vomit.

"Now," a voice said, and Caden died.

The last thing he heard was the Plague bidding him goodbye. "My boy, you've loved me well. Find peace now, for you shall live on in your son."

The last thing he saw, as he struggled to open his eyes, was a pale, indeed translucent boy with black eyes, and the boy was smiling and waving at him, dancing in the air. And where the boy's breath touched the branch of a tree, the leaves crumpled into ashes. Caden – it was the last thing he felt – wished he could wave back.

When the villagers had tied him to the pillar, all they were stoning was a corpse.

Printed in Great Britain
by Amazon